Curious George DISCOVERS

Space

Adaptation by Monica Perez

Based on the TV series teleplay
written by Craig Miller and Joe Fallon

Houghton Mifflin Harcourt

Boston   New York

Photograph on cover (left) © JPL/NASA

Photographs on cover (right) and pp. 5, 7, 11, 13, 17, 18, 23, 25, 26, 27, 28 courtesy of NASA

Photograph on p. 15 courtesy of U.S. Air Force

Photographs on pp. 21, 31, 32 courtesy of HMH/Carrie Garcia

For information about permission to reproduce selections from this book, write to Permissions, Houghton Mifflin Harcourt Publishing Company, 215 Park Avenue South, New York, New York 10003.

ISBN: 978-0-544-50199-7 paper-over-board

ISBN: 978-0-544-50028-0 paperback

Design by Susanna Vagt

www.hmhco.com

Printed in China

SCP 10 9 8 7 6 5 4 3 2 1

4500536762

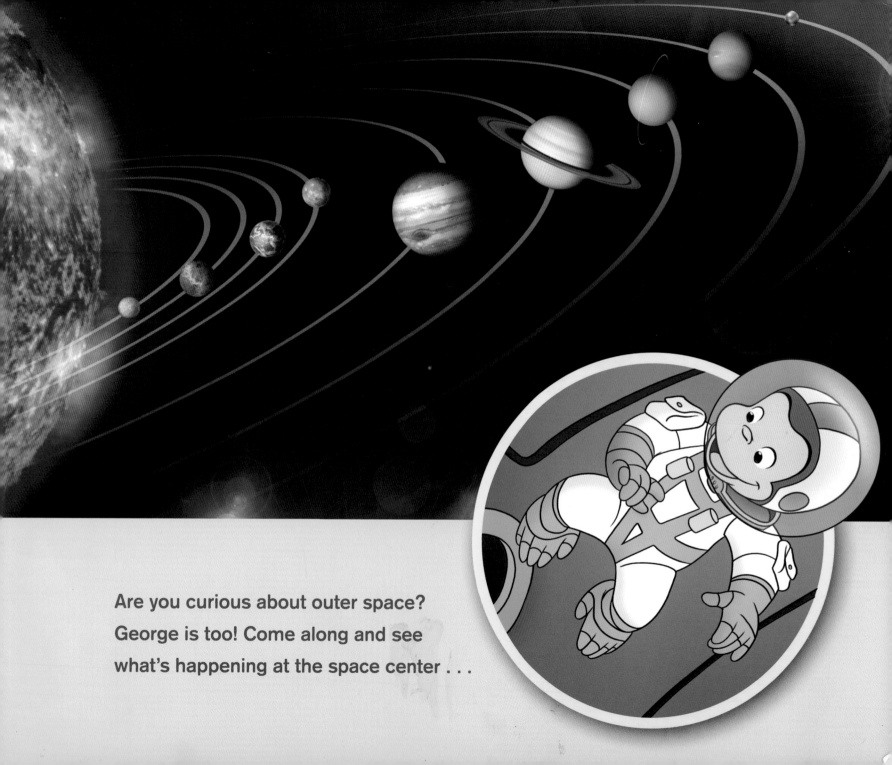

Are you curious about outer space?
George is too! Come along and see
what's happening at the space center . . .

Professor Wiseman invited George and his friend the man with the yellow hat to visit her at the space center. Professor Einstein and Professor Pizza needed help, and she thought they might be able to lend a hand. Or more than one, as it turned out.

"How can we help?" asked the man.

The scientists began to brief the man on his first mission: to restock the space station's food supply. The astronauts on the station had discovered they had only one peanut left to eat.

Did you know . . .
the International Space Station is a spacecraft where astronauts live and do science experiments? The station is as big as a foot-ball field and orbits Earth. Six people can live there at once. A very special thing about the space station is that people from many countries built it and work there together to keep it running.

The man with the yellow hat was planning to ride a space shuttle up through Earth's atmosphere into space. He would enter orbit around Earth and pass near the space station in order to make his delivery. The man would get to experience weightlessness!

How would you like to float inside a spaceship? Of course, George was disappointed he wouldn't be able to come along.

Did you know . . .

that gravity is the force pulling all objects on the surface of a planet toward the center of that planet? It keeps us from floating off into space! Gravity is weaker the farther you are from the center of a planet. If you are far enough away, you are weightless and float.

But in order for the man to release the supplies, he needed to be able to push four buttons at the same time. The man only had two hands. He couldn't do that, but a monkey could. George was thrilled to help!

The hungry scientists on the space station would soon have more than one peanut to eat. George would also deliver some new supplies to help them with science experiments.

"You must launch the payload at exactly the right moment," Professor Einstein said to George. George nodded. He would have to listen to instructions carefully. Do you think that would be hard for one little monkey?

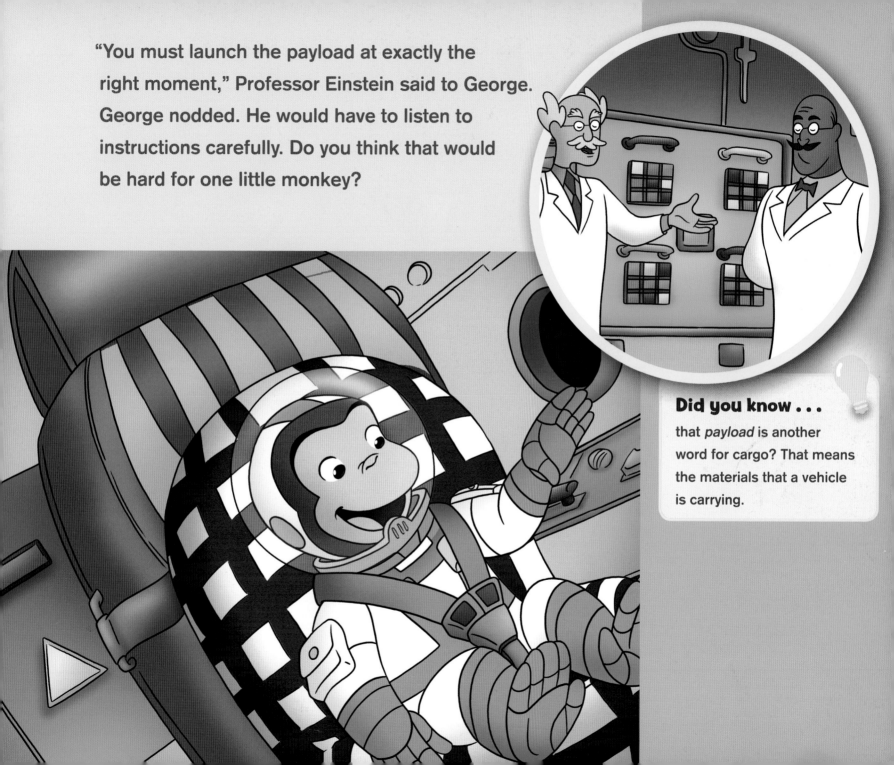

Did you know . . .

that *payload* is another word for cargo? That means the materials that a vehicle is carrying.

Liftoff was a success, but then George wanted to look at the supplies. He took them out to play, but he couldn't get them back inside quickly enough. George missed the payload launch! He passed right by the space station without sending the supplies.

George would have to orbit Earth one more time!

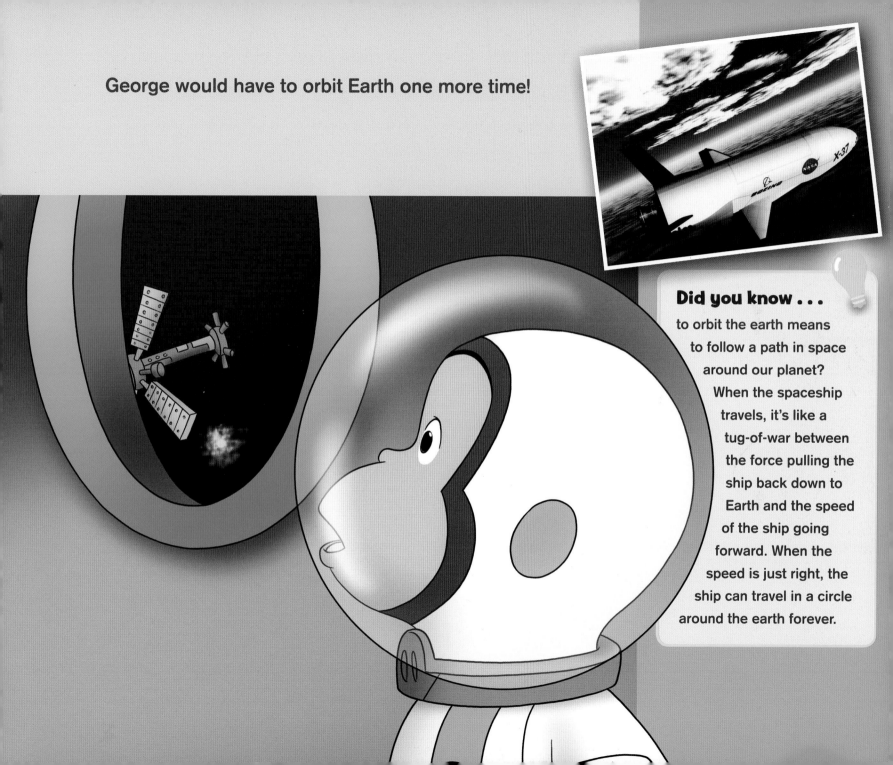

X-37

Did you know . . .
to orbit the earth means to follow a path in space around our planet? When the spaceship travels, it's like a tug-of-war between the force pulling the ship back down to Earth and the speed of the ship going forward. When the speed is just right, the ship can travel in a circle around the earth forever.

"George, you have enough fuel for only one more orbit. You have to get the supplies back in their containers. The next time you pass the station will be the last chance. Then we have to bring you home," warned Professor Wiseman.

George was used to cleaning his room. It was good practice for cleaning up the mess in the spaceship.

He was ready in time to launch the supplies.

Hooray! They made it to the space station!

George had one more task to complete. He had to make it back to the ground safely! To do this the shuttle had to reenter Earth's atmosphere at the right moment.

Did you know . . .

that to land, the shuttle must make a change in direction, which slows the ship down so it falls back to Earth? The ship is coated with a material that can handle the heat created as the ship passes through the atmosphere at such a great speed. The shuttle has a special shape that helps keep it cool and slow it down. It also uses a parachute to slow down safely once it has touched down on the ground.

It was a good thing George listened to instructions this time. He pulled the lever that controlled the ship's direction. He could now land the ship back at the space center. His friends congratulated him on a successful mission!

"On to our next problem . . ." said Professor Pizza, once the shuttle mission was over. "We are having trouble with our Mars rover."

"The controls are getting stuck here at the space center. We are worried that when it actually lands on Mars it will also get stuck on the rocks," added Professor Einstein.

"A Mars rover is a vehicle specially made for exploring the Red Planet and sending information back to Earth," the man explained. "They're testing the new rover here at the space center."

Did you know . . .

Mars is the fourth planet in our solar system? It is smaller and lighter than Earth. Iron oxide, or rust, gives the soil a reddish color, which is why Mars is also known as the Red Planet. Scientists are interested in knowing all about our next-door neighbor in the hope that someday people will be able to visit Mars. Would you like to visit Mars?

George thought the Mars rovers would be fun to drive. But he soon learned that they are operated by remote control only.

Professor Einstein offered everyone a piece of chewing gum as he explained the sticky situation in the space control center.

"You know there's a no-gum rule in here, Einstein," said Professor Pizza.

"Ah, you're right," said Professor Einstein. He opened a large metal drawer and threw his gum out.

George was excited to see the launch of the latest Mars rover. He hoped they could figure out this problem together. They sat around a table to talk and plan.

The man asked, "Since Mars has lower gravity than Earth, is it possible the problem wouldn't even happen there?"

Professor Pizza agreed. "That's certainly possible. If the pull of Earth's gravity is causing the sticking, it might not stick in Mars's low gravity."

"With the lower gravity on Mars, you would be three times stronger there," said Professor Wiseman. "If the rover sticks, maybe we can get it going again by giving it a good push."

George imagined how strong he would be on Mars.

Did you know . . .

that the gravity on Mars is 38 percent of the gravity on Earth? That means that if you weighed 100 pounds on Earth, you would weigh 38 pounds on Mars.

Earth 49.2
Mars 18.696

Test it out!

Using a bathroom scale, weigh yourself. Write the number down. Now ask an adult to help you multiply that number by .38 to get the amount you would weigh on Mars.

George wanted to help, but he was tired and nothing puts a monkey to sleep like a lot of adults talking. The last thing George heard the man saying was "If only we could send someone to Mars to push it . . ."

George fell fast asleep. He dreamed he was going to be the first monkey headed to Mars!

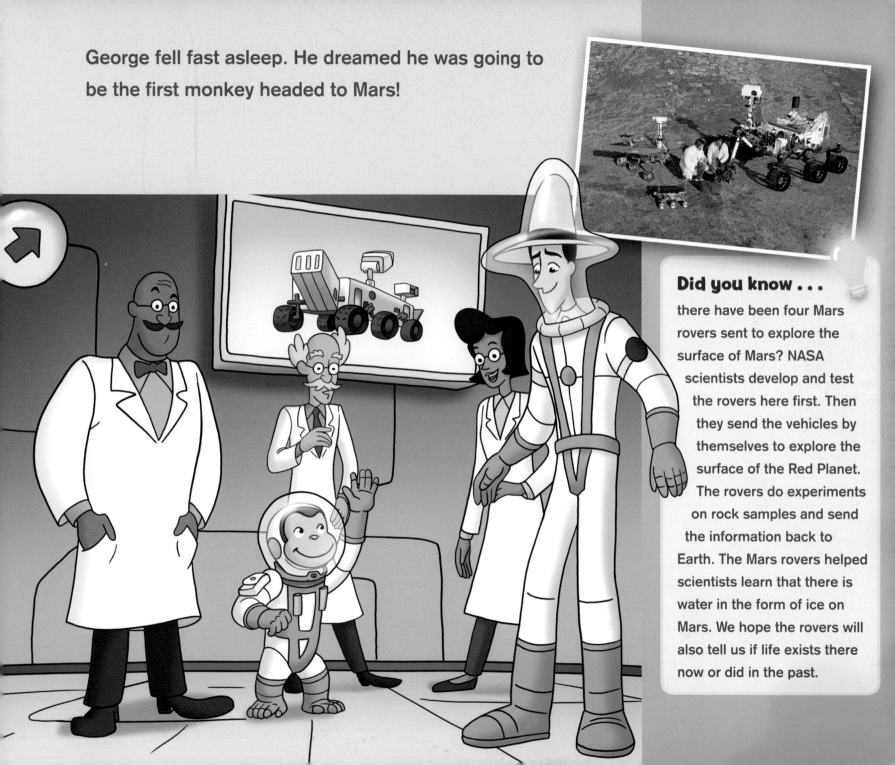

Did you know . . .

there have been four Mars rovers sent to explore the surface of Mars? NASA scientists develop and test the rovers here first. Then they send the vehicles by themselves to explore the surface of the Red Planet. The rovers do experiments on rock samples and send the information back to Earth. The Mars rovers helped scientists learn that there is water in the form of ice on Mars. We hope the rovers will also tell us if life exists there now or did in the past.

In his dream, Professor Wiseman told him, "It's an important mission, George. If the rover sticks, your job is to give it a good push."

The man was going on the space mission with George—how lucky! George wouldn't be lonely on his trip.

When the ship finally landed on Mars, George was sitting on top of the Mars rover. When it was released, he went with it! The rover bounced along the surface of the Red Planet. George was on a runaway vehicle!

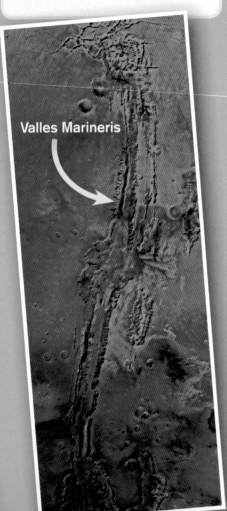

Valles Marineris

Lucky for George, he found the remote that controlled the rover. He was able to slow down the rover. Whew. He also had a book about the Mars terrain. Now he could explore Mars!

George rolled up to a very deep, very wide valley that looked like the Grand Canyon, only much larger. The book told him it was called the Valles Marineris.

George also found the Olympus Mons, the highest volcano in our solar system. It had a great view. He wished his friend could enjoy it too.

At least George could see where his rocket had landed. He began to drive the rover back toward the spaceship.

Olympus Mons

Did you know . . .

the Olympus Mons is 16 miles (25 km) high, three times the height of Mount Everest? It is one of many volcanoes on Mars that erupted for millions of years but are no longer active.

But that's when the rover got stuck. George opened a panel and discovered great big globs of green gum were clogging up the controls! No wonder it kept sticking.

Luckily, in the low gravity of Mars, George was able to use his superstrength to pick up the vehicle and carry it back to the ship.

Did you know . . .

that names of the Mars rovers have been Sojourner (which means "traveler"), Opportunity, Spirit, and Curiosity? Isn't Curiosity a good name for a Mars rover for George? What would you name your own Mars rover?

That was when George woke up from his dream! Now he knew why the real Mars rover was getting stuck.

He led the scientists back to the control room and pointed out a gummed-up panel. Professor Einstein had been using the rover control system as a trash bin by accident! "Oops," the professor said.

Do you think the Mars rover was able to launch after all? After the control panel had been cleaned, of course!

"It's a good thing monkeys are dreamers," the man said. George agreed. He had many dreams as big as the one about traveling to Mars. Next stop: Pluto!

One Great Gravity Experiment

What does a cup full of water have in common with a spaceship? Find out with this experiment.

You will need . . .

- **a disposable cup**
- **a pen or pencil to poke a hole in the cup**
- **water**
- **an outdoor area, or your bathtub**

What to do:

1. With the help of an adult, poke a hole in the side of the cup.
2. Cover the hole with your thumb and fill the cup with water.

3. Hold the cup up high and uncover the hole. You'll see that the water flows out steadily. This is one reason why it's good to do this experiment outdoors or over a bathtub!

Now, what do you think would happen if you let go of the cup? Would the water flow faster or slower out of the cup?

4. Cover the hole with your thumb and fill the cup with water again.
5. Hold the cup up high again, and this time, let it drop! The water stays in the cup as it falls.

What's going on? An explanation of "free fall" and "weightlessness"

When you're holding the cup, gravity pulls down on both the cup and water. But the only thing that moves is the water, because you keep the cup in place. This is the same as a spacecraft on the ground. Gravity holds the spacecraft in place, and the astronauts down on the floor. If there was a hole in the bottom of the spacecraft, the poor astronauts would fall right through, just like the water did!

It's a different story when you drop the cup. Gravity pulls down on the cup and the water equally and they fall at the same speed. The scientific term for this is free fall. This is like a spacecraft in orbit: the spacecraft and the astronauts are both constantly in free fall, and the astronauts experience weightlessness and float.

Planet Picnic

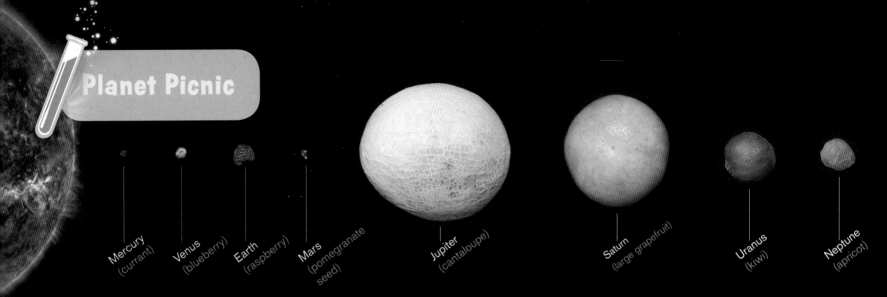

Mercury (currant) · Venus (blueberry) · Earth (raspberry) · Mars (pomegranate seed) · Jupiter (cantaloupe) · Saturn (large grapefruit) · Uranus (kiwi) · Neptune (apricot)

In order to understand how big each planet is compared to Earth, you can use fruit!

- Look in your kitchen or go to the grocery store to find one of each fruit in this chart. The chart shows the diameter of each planet divided by a billion. Diameter is the line that passes from one side of a planet to the other side.

- Line the fruits up in order and snap a picture.

- You'll notice that the last four planets are much bigger than the first four. The last four planets are called "gas giants" because their surface is made of a gas. The first four planets have solid, rocky surfaces.

Now comes the best part—chop your fruit up and enjoy an out-of-this-world fruit salad!

Planet	Diameter / billion (mm=millimeters)	Fruit stand-in
Mercury	4.9 mm	Currant or elderberry
Venus	12.1 mm	Blueberry
Earth	12.8 mm	Raspberry
Mars	6.8 mm	Pomegranate seed or raisin
Jupiter	143 mm	Cantaloupe
Saturn	120.5 mm	Large grapefruit
Uranus	51.1 mm	Kiwi or small plum
Neptune	49.5 mm	Apricot